THE

BABYSITTER

ANGEL NGWASEH

First published in Great Britain in 2020 by Likambi Global Publishing

Copyright: 2020 by Angel Ngwaseh

www.likambiglobalpublishing.com

ISBN: 978-1-913266-97-4

CHAPTERS

CHAPTER 1

One more hour until my *baby*sitter comes..."Mum! Why can't Liam look after me?" I complained. "He's sixteen and I'm twelve, which means he is technically *and* legally allowed to care for me!" Mum didn't care though. She just chuckled and went on eating her enormous breakfast.

"Don't worry, sweetheart, you may be with her every day, but you still get to see me once a day."

What my mum meant was that she and her friends had decided that it would be fun for them to have a whole month to themselves without disturbance from us kids, but that didn't change the fact that I was going to be with an annoying lady who probably was going to ruin all my fun throughout the holidays.

"You also know I can't trust Liam after last year when I left you guys at home. He totally proved to me how amateur he is and how he's not even able to take care of his precious sister," Mum ranted whilst staring at Liam whose head was held down.

"It was amazing though," he whispered under his breath, a faint smirk under his nose. Short story short, last year, when Mum left us at home, Liam, thinking that he was so cool, went and told every single one of his classmates about what Mum had done, which led to all of his friends somehow managing to convince him to have a party. This meant that I was going to have a bunch of year elevens in my house! But should I tell you the worst part, I didn't get to participate and it's not that I wanted to, but, seriously, that didn't mean they had to lock me in the basement. Firstly, it was cold in there and, secondly, I was all alone in that dusty, dark room.

"Like honestly, Liam! Your sister could've died of starvation or lack of comfort," announced mum finally as she gave me a choking hug.

"Oh, and I nearly forgot, because of your reckless behaviour, you will be helping pack for every single activity I go on with my friends and—" But before she could finish her sentence, the doorbell rang. No. It wasn't the postman. It was Violet...

CHAPTER 2

"Lora! I have finally arrived!" shrieked a shrill voice from outside the door. My mum waited for me to stand up and go open the front door but I never did. I didn't even budge.

I wasn't going to open the door for someone I didn't even want to meet. After a couple of seconds, I gave up with my mum and grimly walked to the door. I could feel my hand dripping with sweat, which felt rather disgusting. Each one of my fingers was trembling with fear. I opened it, staring uncontrollably. I mean I know it's rude to, but she just didn't look ... well ... *normal.* She wore a wide straw hat and a rather odd colour of sunglasses. Her hands were covered with thick gloves. Liam came over to see what was taking us so long and, when he arrived, he suddenly knew why.

"Aren't you MELTING in that?" he howled behind me. Violet, who was supposed to be babysitting us, was quite taken aback by how she was welcomed.

"Well, little boy—"

"Actually I'm sixteen," said Liam quietly.

"I do not care how old you are! You still have no right to ask why I have ... layers of clothes on. I mean you can never be too prepared for rain, snow, hail or even a thunderstorm!"

I stood there quietly but not peacefully. There was something about this lady that just did not seem right. I mean aren't babysitters supposed to look normal in a way? I just didn't understand one bit of it. I thought my mum would only befriend someone who didn't leave a trail of sweat wherever they waddled like a snail. And when I say that, I am NOT exaggerating! You could see the salty water leaking through all the clothing, which made everything unsightly.

CHAPTER 3

"Nice to see you again, Violet. I know it must have been a long journey, but don't worry; I've made you some coffee and cookies. By the way, if you need me, I'll be upstairs packing my clothes. Liam, you've got to help me, remember."

I definitely did not want to be left alone with *this* lady. "Mum, I'll come and help. It's fine, Liam, you can stay here." I raced up the stairs into my mum's room and started gasping for air.

"Have you all of a sudden turned into a dog?" My mum chuckled.

"Actually, I have not. I came here to—"

"I knew you didn't want to help pack."

"Yes, I know. Sorry, it's just that I don't trust that Violet woman downstairs. It's like she's in the Antarctic! Please can you postpone your *Girls' Month Out* and stay home instead? Auntie Linda is coming next month!"

I know when my mum can sense that I'm panicking and this was definitely one of those moments. She sighed and crouched next to me.

"I know that you don't trust her, but that is because you haven't known her for as long as I have." I glared at Mum smirking for I knew for a fact that she had only met Violet seven months ago and visited her house exactly twice.

"Okay. I don't know her *that* well, but I do know her well enough to leave you and Liam with her for only five weeks. Plus, you'll get to see me nearly every day before I set off for the next adventure with the girls, but, most importantly, be respectful, okay?"

I did have to admit my mum did a pretty good job of persuading me into calming down and believing that Violet was alright. Not that I trusted her entirely; I mean she was still pretty weird. Like when I came back downstairs, the lounge seemed to look a lot dimmer than usual; then I figured out why. Someone had shut all the windows and finally removed all her layers till she finally poured out of the penultimate coat. She had soft brown shoulder-length hair with faint blonde highlights. And as for her eyes, they were a pale hazel beneath her arched eyebrows. On her ears were multiple piercings that all seemed to have birds on them. She didn't look extraordinary at all underneath all that layering; if anything, she looked like an ordinary human.

CHAPTER 4

I gave my mum a hug, which apparently to her was a hug that you would get from a wild forest bear trying to strangle you. Vicky started to get impatient and was yelling out of the car window telling my mum to hurry up. My mum gave Liam and me a kiss on the cheek and ran down the front door steps into Vicky's car. We all waved. We turned to face Violet just to see her grinning all weird like and to be honest I was starting to think that even Liam was getting quite uncomfortable. I'm not really sure, but I think she could sense the fact that we were starting to back away, so she stopped smirking and chuckled nervously.

"I'm sorry for making you feel a bit scared, but to be honest I'm as nervous as you!" We looked at her rather confused.

"I'm only twenty-four and I have *never* babysat anyone and this is my very first time." I was very taken aback by this because my mum is thirty-four and that is a ten-year difference. I was just about to question how they met, but she shut me down quickly. I could tell by Liam's face that he was going to attempt to trick her into thinking that he was allowed to march around wherever he pleased, so of course I took care of that.

"Violet, my mum said that you should not let Liam out of the house if an adult is not supervising him and I understand if you don't believe me but you can check with my mum."

I said it with so much pride that I was pleased to see Liam glaring at me. I smirked and purposely nudged him. It wasn't the best nudge because Liam is surprisingly tall.

"Alright now, settle down. I don't want to have to call your mother just now."

After the mini conversation with Violet, she left the room. I didn't know what to do at that point so I strolled up to my room. Then I thought of something that made me shut my door frantically. I didn't know what Violet would think of my room at all! I especially thought she wouldn't like it because my brother always made fun of me for having a pink room. Firstly, that is very stereotypical and secondly, there is nothing wrong with pink! Every time he walked past my room and the door was open, he would always criticise me and say that it was a baby colour and people would make fun of me for having a toddler room. It would always get to me even though I tried to take no notice of it. I sat on my king-sized bed and thought about what I could do to get my mind off this subject. Then it occurred to me that I should help Violet know what she was doing whilst babysitting us, like a guide book. Yes! A guide book. I dashed to my desk and got out all my arts and crafts to get started.

I worked on this guide for like an hour and even snuck into my brother's room and pinched one of his hole punchers, but before returning it, I painted it pink just to finally feel the meaning of *revenge is sweet*. Once I finished it, I headed downstairs to catch Violet watching a very intimidating vampire movie. No one in the history of my life has watched this series and I was so shocked that I nearly dropped the guide book in my hands.

"AAAHH!" I screamed hysterically, which made Violet wake up from her nap. She looked at me then glared at the TV. She snatched the remote off the coffee table and switched the TV off.

"I am so sorry. I have no idea how t-that got on." I contemplated her every move until she came up to me to see what I wanted. She glanced down at the book and so did I.

"I made y-you this. Just in case you got a bit lost during your stay here."

She grabbed it from my hands and nodded to me as a thank you. I didn't know what to say to her for I was too frightened. I started to back away slowly and then, when she turned around, I raced to Liam's room.

***

"What are you doing here?" he snapped, unplugging his headphones. I gasped for breath and walked up to him shaking him frantically.

"Do you know that creepy vampire series that nobody watches?"

"Yes. What about it?" he questioned hesitantly.

"Well, I just caught Violet accidentally watching it, or so I thought, but I still think she put it on deliberately. Don't you think that's a bit suspicious?" Liam released his phone from his clutches; his mouth opened wide. He shook his head intensely and then looked at *me* suspiciously.

"Are you sure it's not just your imagination? Wait! Are you trying to trick me?" I was outraged at this point. I only lie if I desperately have to, which is almost never! I glared at him coldly and grabbed his hand with so much force he started yelling at me to loosen up. I told him to shut up and tiptoed into the lounge whilst Violet made us some dinner. I snagged the remote and turned on the TV to prove to Liam that she was definitely watching that ghoulish show. Liam's mouth must have dropped all the way to the floor and rolled across the street. He didn't even say anything; he just shook his hand off me and took off to his room shutting his door loudly. Violet ran out of the kitchen and into the lounge.

"What happened? Is anyone hurt?"

I shook my head and smiled nervously, trying to seem as innocent as ever. I really started to have my suspicions about her...

CHAPTER 5

For the rest of the day I stayed in my bed, curled up in a tight ball. I sat like that for a few minutes until I remembered something. I had forgotten to feed my hamster. I should have asked my mum earlier if we could stop by the shops and get her food. Sadly, I forgot to, but at least there was an adult at home, although I really didn't feel like approaching Violet. I mean she still gave me the creeps, and I had no idea what was in store for me.

I was still debating what to do when Liam waltzed into my room. I can't even remember half of what happened in that moment. The part that I can recall is when I aimed my pillow at Liam for coming into my room, but the result that I earned was the pillow crashing into Violet's face. She stared at me; her eyes as red as blood. I swear I picked up a hushed hiss. I panicked and shuffled further towards the corner of my wall, hoping that I would sink into it and evaporate into a little puddle. I guess she must have realised that she was acting oddly so she exhaled deeply and walked away silently; so did Liam. I sprang underneath my covers as sour tears streamed down my face. I really wanted to talk to my mum. I quietly wept, praying that some sort of miracle would happen. I mopped my face, although it was still blotchy and my eyes were swollen. I rubbed them repeatedly so that I could make my way to Lollie's cage.

I conscientiously picked her out of her sloppy pen. It was in desperate need of a clean-up, but I couldn't worry about that now. I nestled her up to my chest. As I did this, Violet sauntered into my room all gloomy like. "I am so sorry, Lexi, if I scared you. I hope you don't think that I'm w-weird it's just that my contacts are a new design, which c-change colour d-depending on my moods." She chuckled nervously.

I wasn't convinced at all, so I just asked, "So were you angry at me in that moment? Because I'm positive that your eyes turned red." I only said that because when her eyes had turned red, I felt like they had pierced through my heart for a second. She looked at me restlessly as if she was guilty of a crime. I think she was looking for a reasonable excuse for what I just said. She raised her hand until she just gave in and tiptoed away. Now I was *definitely* scared. I mean I had every right to be. Who gets contacts that change color depending on their mood? Why would she apologize to me after like forty-five minutes when I thought she would have forgotten already? It did not add up at all.

CHAPTER 6

At the end of the day, I devoured my supper then went upstairs to brush my teeth. As I finished, I glanced at the door and what I saw made me splash my cup of water all over myself. Violet was taking *out* her teeth. Now, I know people are going to say, "Maybe she just needs dentures," but I know what I saw. I am one hundred percent sure that she had needle-like fangs in her mouth. I swung my head from side to side to try to take my mind off what I saw. As soon as I did this, I came back to life again and felt my clothes sinking into me. I rushed into my room and changed out of my drenched outfit and got my pyjamas on before nuzzling into my bed. Then I had this weird feeling in my head. I can't really remember what made my hair stand on end, but I ended up covering my face and adjusted a hole at the side to breathe.

***

The very next day, after getting dressed and all that, I darted down the stairs for the exquisite pancakes that lay on the table and what escalated next was horrifying. As I was dragging my chair out from the table, I noticed something on Liam's neck; it looked like teeth marks. Really bloody teeth marks—well, dried blood. I was so startled that I accidentally splashed Violet in the face with my drink. How many times was I going to drop my drink on someone? I have never in my life seen someone get bitten and when I say that, I mean in live action. I definitely do not want to, but that wasn't even the problem. There were bite marks on Liam's neck! But the question was how did they get there?

CHAPTER 7

The whole thing was mortifying! Liam looked at me confused as he carried on munching on his food.

"What's wrong, Lexi?" asked Violet, turning off the tap. I managed to point my quivering hand towards the ghastly sight. I turned to face Violet and she definitely looked nervous with a hint of guilt; almost as if *she* had something to do with this. Her eyes widened and she turned paler than ever. I hoped one of us would come back to our senses and do something, but we just stood there. I finally grew impatient and said, "Maybe it would help if we grabbed a wet cloth or something." I was expecting Violet to come back to life, but she carried on staring.

"Hello?" Eventually, I was able to earn her attention just before she grabbed a towel and asked Liam to dab it on his neck.

***

I tried to relax for the upcoming hours but I couldn't. Something kept haunting me every time I blinked, let alone closed my eyes. I finally ended up in Liam's room. I knew he would yell at me any moment to get out, but whilst I was there, I took the opportunity to ask him something. "Whilst you were sleeping, did you feel anything tingly on your neck?" He shook his head and in an instant it turned into a nod. Liam slowly stood up and shut his eyes. They were still closed when he said, "I was on my phone at one a.m.—"

"You were on your phone past bedtime!" I yelled.

Liam put his finger to his mouth and hissed, "Shh. Do you want to know what happened?" I nodded leisurely.

"Okay. So, as I was saying, I was on my phone at around one and then I heard footsteps quietly walking towards my room. I hid my phone under my pillow and closed my eyes tightly. I could hear someone breathing down my neck, which made the whole thing very tense. Then, all of a sudden, the person's hand yanked at the collar of my pyjamas. Their breathing got heavier and heavier. Louder and louder. Then something sharp pierced into my neck. I had to stay quiet or I was sure to get caught. I didn't think much about it."

The whole thing was so appalling that I wanted to throw up. But then it dawned on me. With the exception of me, the only other person in the house was Violet...

CHAPTER 8

My whole body was aching in agony, shivers slithering down my spine. I had just got a tiny bit used to my babysitter to find out she could be a blood-thirsty vampire! Not that I was one hundred percent sure, but you get what I mean. I was panting hysterically, wondering if I would suffocate. I told Liam how I felt and, for once, he agreed with me. We stood there in consternation. A lady who had been looking after us for just one or two days could be or possibly was a vampire. I was so glad my mum was coming over to check up on us before going to Jenny's. I prayed that she would come over any moment now.

The doorbell rang. I streaked downstairs and yanked at the door. My mum had a wide smile on her face before hugging me as tightly as always. She looked at Liam and pinched his cheek even though she knew he despised it. "Good afternoon, my little buttercups. I hope you've had a great time so far. Anyway, where is Violet?"

Liam and I exchanged worried looks. We didn't know whether my mum knew that Violet was clandestinely a vampire. I hate keeping confidential information as bad as this from my mum so I just blurted out, "Mum! I think your friend, Violet, is a vampire!"

She looked at me baffled as if I had spoken a foreign language. "Pardon?"

"I said I think Violet is a vampire."

"I think your dreams are getting the better of you, sweetheart. Or maybe you guys were playing dress-ups, which is totally unlikely. WAIT! Are you feeling sick?"

No. I was not *only* sick, I felt very lightheaded. I felt like if I stopped breathing for even one second, I was going to collapse. I felt like I couldn't even eat anything in my own house because it could be infected. The thought of having something like blood in our food made me turn green. Violet finally walked in and gave my mum a great, long hug. I gulped. To be honest, I started to get really exasperated because my mum had no idea that her so-called *friend* was definitely a vampire. How was she okay to leave us with this vile creature? I stayed quiet though. I didn't want to look like a fool, although I wasn't! My theory made perfect sense. I needed to alert my mum.

CHAPTER 9

I opened my mouth to call out Violet but shut it again. I knew my mum would just laugh it off and then Violet would probably punish me. Or even worse! I did not want any trouble, although I think this is where the burden may have begun. My mum hurriedly packed her swimsuit then rushed out the front door for another adventure. I really wanted to go with her. Maybe even leave the country to stay away from Violet. I now could feel her breathing down my neck too. I prayed that she wouldn't damage every single one of my bones. I started to ponder. *Did she hear what I said about her? Does she know that Liam and I don't feel comfortable with her?* All these questions racing around my head like a Ferris wheel. The pain I felt when I found out that my *baby*sitter was possibly a vampire was back again. It stung even more now. My whole body was bubbling up like a tank. It wasn't because I was angry but because I was terrified. I thought that my belly was going to explode at any second.

She slowly placed her hand on my shoulder and gripped on to it securely. I turned around a full three hundred and sixty degrees just to see her expression. To my surprise, she had a lovely smile on her face. I had just about calmed down when I noticed her *dentures*. *Again.* Just something about them made me want to gag, especially because she was using them for non-dental reasons, to hide her identity.

CHAPTER 10

She leaned in to give me a hug, but I dodged it. Yes, that might've been rude, but would you do that with a vampire? I could tell by her frown that she was not pleased with my physical response, so I searched my brain for a reasonable justification. This took me at least a minute or so.

"Oh, I'm so sorry, Violet, it's just that I have a very unpleasant cold and I definitely wouldn't want to pass it on to a wonderful babysitter." I tentatively walked to the kitchen right after I noticed that her upside-down smile and had moved by a one-hundred-and-eighty-degree angle to a mammoth grin. I needed proof. I needed verification so that my mum could understand that I was right. I swiftly and briefly checked each cabinet in search of at least a jar of blood or something that a vampire might use. After about thirty minutes I gave up and burst into tears. My life was probably unstable. I did not want to have three thousand bite marks all over my body. I had to think of a way to blackmail her or even just find a way to get my mum to realise that Violet was a vampire.

***

The very next day, I am pretty sure I barely said anything for most of the morning, but in order for me to devise an agile plan to prove me right I was going to need someone's help. Someone I wasn't very fond of. Someone who would only be concerned with any of my conversations if they had anything to do with him or his safety. Someone who loved to torment me in every way possible. Liam...

CHAPTER 11

It took me quite some time to come to the conclusion of asking Liam, but to be honest he is sixteen and is a *bit* wiser than me when it comes to assembling a crafty plan.

"Hey Liam. I need you to set up a plan so that we can confirm that Violet is a vampire. Cool? Thanks."

"Slow your roll. I never agreed to this and, in addition to that, we never signed a special contract saying that you can boss me around *and* I think you're forgetting I'm older—"

"Which is why I need your help." At this point, instead of a *how dare you come in my room* face I received a more bewildered look like a *what on earth are you talking about* face. I couldn't really blame him because anyone would have had that exact reaction.

"Because you're older and have a more developed brain, I think, I will need your help constructing something to take Violet down and show Mum that I'm not an insane twelve-year-old girl with a strange imagination."

"Okay. Other than you using difficult words and you insulting me in your so-called speech, how does that benefit me?"

I gave him the stink eye. Why does he always want something when I ask him for a favour? By the way, this wasn't only going to help me; I'm pretty sure Liam would thank me for the next forty-eight hours if we accomplished this mastermind plan.

We wrote; we drew; we brainstormed all afternoon. Well, almost all afternoon. We had to stop for a little while when my mum came in to check up on us *and* we also had to stop when we heard the front door slam ... shut. Yet again, we exchanged sceptical looks. We must have had the same thoughts because we sprang out of our chairs and ran to the front driveway, searching to see if Violet was in sight. Then

Liam pointed across the street and yelled, "LOOK! SHE'S ENTERING HER CAR!"

We both bolted to the other side of the street and, fortunately for us, the back trunk was unlocked so we clambered in. It was a very tight rear boot, which gives you an impression of how small her car was. Leaping into the back of somebody's car was not a thoroughly thought out thought, so when I whispered, "Why are we squished in the back of Violet's car not knowing where she's going and how long she might be there for?" Liam rolled his eyes as well as moving his elbow to a much more spacious area.

"Well, I thought maybe we could video tape some evidence. Like maybe she's going to get vampire stuff. Or-or some illegal substance!"

I had no idea what was going on inside his bizarre brain so I asked, "Well, if even if she does, I don't think she'll be too happy to see two kids spying on her if she checks in here!"

"How do you know she's going to check in here, Miss Know-It-All?" I was actually starting to wonder what goes on in Liam's bizarre brain.

"I think everyone who enters the city is going to bring some paid-for items to their car and put them in their trunk." From then on, we kept on arguing back and forth very silently but had to stop when the car jerked into a halt.

As soon as Violet's door shut, Liam and I scampered out of the trunk and followed her, trying to look as innocent as possible to passers-by. We followed her down past the popular brands, across the fast-food restaurants and up by the supermarkets until we came across a dark alley. Just like every other eerie alley, it was extremely moist. Nasty, sticky moist. Everything was silent apart from the dripping of who knows what and the tips of Violet's high heels sinking to the ground with every step. She turned a corner along the graffiti-covered wall whilst Liam and I pressed our back against it. The dampness of it made me want to puke. Liam put his index finger to his mouth so that, with us not speaking, we could better hear the muffled speaking. There was only one problem with the talking. Both voices kind of sounded similar so it was hard to tell which one was which.

"How much for the pack of blood?"

"I'll give it to yah for fifty quid."

"You want fifty pounds for five packs of blood? I need this to keep me alive! How come the other times I came here the other girl gave them to me for ten pounds?"

"Keep yah bloomin' voice down! If it can keep yah alive then it's worth that fifty quid, yah hear me? A tenner for every jar now. So, if yah want to keep livin' then give me my fifty quid that I deserve!" There was a long silence led by a long sigh then a shuffle of I think money being handed over.

Liam had already got ready to leave and started beckoning me to follow him to the car. As we were walking, something popped into my head.

"Do you think Violet was the one who needed the human blood?"

"Of course she did! Why do you think we think she's a vampire? Plus, the second voice had a different type of accent." We needed to gather just one more piece of evidence. Hopefully that would be enough...

CHAPTER 12

As soon as we got home, and Violet was out of sight, Liam and I scurried out of the trunk and sprinted to the front door. We jiggled with the door knob but it just wouldn't budge. Violet must've locked it. Slimy sweat sliding down to the ground.

"Oi! Is that you, Lexi?" blared a not-so-recognisable voice. I jumped with so much force that the door jolted open. I took a quick glance at the mysterious voice to find my school teacher. I knew what the next question was going to be. I grabbed Liam's hand and shut the front door. Breathlessly, we sluggishly ambled to the lounge. There on the sofa was Violet, watching the spine-chilling vampire series yet again.

"AAAHHH!!!" we screeched.

"AAAHHH!" Violet hollered. "W-what! I thought you guys were in bed!" she protested whilst hurriedly switching off the TV. My heart was racing. So were my feet. There was no time to lose. We had to find somewhere to hide and quick.

Concealed in the closet underneath the stair, being jammed in a small area with Liam was not pleasant, especially when there was a VAMPIRE on the loose. "Come on, kids, I'm not going t-to bite. I think. It'll only be a tiny little nibble or shall I say cut. Ooh. Maybe we can compromise and play hide 'n' seek. Where are you guys?" hooted Violet in a horrible convivial voice. I could hear a lot of smashing and clattering of household essentials and an ear-splitting cackle. Thoughts pounding in my head. None of them were any use. We were surely going to be put into her bloody pie or something.

"Well, what are we going to do now, Liam?" I whispered.

"Right. We need to find a way to sneak into the back garden—"

"Excuse me! It's late and dark. We'll end up running straight into a lamppost!" I snapped in a low voice.

"You're going to have to listen to me even though it's going to be risky." We both gulped.

"Ooh. Is that whispering I hear? Don't worry, children. If you weren't snooping around in my business, I wouldn't have to do this, although I love turning into a bat!" hissed Violet.

"Okay, let's go through the back." We both slithered around to the exit at the back and clambered out to Liam's fort.

"And what now, you fool? We can't just hide here till sunrise, Liam!" He shushed me and we waited there for thirty minutes or so.

Now I could hear the fluttering of Violet's wings around us. "Where are you two children? I might be able add a few jars of blood WHEN YOU COME OUT!"

"Okay Lexi. Now pull that string that's dangling in the corner. That should protect us." I pulled the rope securely. A few tins collapsed at the other side of the garden. "Oh. So, you've decided to let me get you. For you, very unwise; for me, excellent. NOW BLEED SO THE PROCESS WON'T BE SO PAINFUL!"

Liam started beckoning me to me to drag a lever, which activated a stuffed-up balloon to hit Violet, aka the bat. There was a loud thud and something clattered to the ground.

"OW! WHICH ONE OF YOU DEMONS HIT ME?"

Demon? Demon? She was a demon who was trying to murder kids!

I curled up into a tiny ball, clutching on to a rough pillow.

"Well, don't just stay there like a baby; help me throw the rotten tomatoes at her!" retorted Liam quietly.

Instead of questioning why he had rotten tomatoes in his fort I slowly grabbed one. It felt very soggy and smelt like years old compost that hadn't been cleaned out by the owner or worms. We threw a few and then I stopped. That could give us away. Plus, I didn't like the feeling at all of mouldy old tomatoes in my hands. A loud squelching came from a few meters back. She must have turned back into a human or something.

"RIGHT! I'VE HAD ENOUGH OF CHASING YOU BRATS AROUND! I'LL JUST HAVE TO RIP YOU GUYS UP LIMB BY LIMB! GET OUT!" I was completely ready to wail out a scream. I needed my mum.

"So, the next plan is to get her in the basement beneath the stairs and lock her in there till mum comes."

"And how exactly are we going to do that?"

"I brought a jar of blood. We could make a trail and get her to follow it to the basement!"

WOW! He could have thought of that in the first place. I just hoped it wasn't going to be as hard as it sounded...

CHAPTER 13

"The current problem is how are we going to make a trail of blood?" I enquired. "You do know that vampires have super vision or something."

He put his hand to his chin like many people do when they are thinking extremely hard. I was still waiting to hear Liam's plan.

"Oksy. So I know how good you are at imitating other people and using different accents, so you're going to pretend to be our neighbour wandering in the dark and I'm going to pour the blood all the way to closet."

I had to admit, Liam was actually being relevant for the first time in ages. I had to clamber through the passageway and get into character. I sneaked through the front door and back through our neighbour's back garden.

"Hi love! What yah doin' out here?" I questioned in a chirpy tone. Violet's blood-red eyes pierced through my heart and I almost broke character. Her veins were popping out; I thought they were going to burst. Her skin was pale and her teeth were as sharp as a knife's blade.

"You look lost. Yah need 'elp?" I said in the same cheerful manner. The gritted teeth expression that *was* on her face suddenly changed into a broad grin.

"Well, kind of. Do you happen to know where two kids could be? I'm meant to be babysitting them, but they keep hiding from me. Such brats!" I decided not to protest against being classed as a *brat!*

"Well, I haven't seen them, but if I do, I'll contact you right away."

By now, I reckoned, Liam must've have poured enough blood for a whole nation to see. I waved and waddled back to the front door. I took off all the character role clothes and waited for the right moment to shut the closet door. Loud sniffs were becoming more thorough and irritating as well as the loud cracking of the floorboards beneath Violet's purple slippers.

"Okay, when she enters, *both* of us shut it as tightly as possible, alright?" I nodded vigorously as sweat was hurled everywhere. A loud gulp and a hydrated sigh came from the closet.

"NOW!" We barred the door firmly.

"LET ME OUT NOW, YOU DEMON CHILDREN!"

Just then, I remembered something.

"Liam, there's a window there! She'll burn to a crisp at sunlight," I whispered sharply.

"And? That's what we want to happen, right?"

We got a lot of household objects and merged them together to barricade the door. After that, we dashed upstairs and locked our doors.

***

When the sun was finally beaming, someone knocked loudly on my door. I rubbed my eyes forcefully and climbed out of bed. Liam stumbled into my room and whispered, "Let's go and see what happened to Violet." I hesitantly walked downstairs, careful not to produce noise. We cautiously opened the door and what stood before us was worth laughing our heads off. Instead of Violet ready to lunge at us or even pounce was a huge clump ash that lay there silently; not a movement in place. We laughed until we fell to the ground. The front door opened wildly.

"Hello buttercups! How has your day been?"

We both rushed to our mum and hugged her extremely tightly.

"OH! You guys never hug me this tightly. Besides the point, where's Violet?"

We both exchanged anxious looks. What were we going to say to fool Mum?

"Well..."

"Well, V-Violet left overnight and umm..."

"She said she wanted to move country and that we should tell you that she was done and doesn't want you to contact her or anything."

The flabbergasted look on my mum's face was probably all the evidence we needed that she must've believed us.

"Oh, okay then. I guess I'm going to have to call your Aunty Linda to come earlier." She chuckled. As she walked out the room, dialling our aunt's number, we both let out a huge sigh we had been restraining all morning. We tossed the ash and revolting blood in the dumpster and forgot about it forever. But we never knew when we could encounter another mysterious creature...

www.ingramcontent.com/pod-product-compliance
Lightning Source LLC
Chambersburg PA
CBHW070453170726
48291CB00005B/1741